GOD
ONLY
KNOWS

GOD ONLY KNOWS

THE SONYA WATKINS STORY

LATONIA NARELLE HENDERSON

ARCHWAY PUBLISHING

Archway Publishing books may be ordered through booksellers or by contacting:

Archway Publishing
1663 Liberty Drive
Bloomington, IN 47403
www.archwaypublishing.com
1 (888) 242-5904

ISBN: 978-1-4808-8053-5 (sc)
ISBN: 978-1-4808-8054-2 (e)

Library of Congress Control Number: 2019909370

Print information available on the last page.

Archway Publishing rev. date: 9/24/2019

DEDICATION

To my two beautiful daughters, Jasmin and Jewel, thank you for allowing me to speak wisdom into your lives. You two young ladies make me proud to be your mother. The sky is the limit, ladies. Follow your dreams.

To my beloved late Bishop Nathaniel Holcomb and to my Pastor Valerie Ivy Holcomb, thank you for investing in my life. Your teachings and love helped me through a very trying time in my life. I could have been Sonya, but you taught me that the love of God is like no other love in this world.

To my good friends. You know exactly who you are. I love and thank you for being who you are. No one can take your place in my heart. May our friendship remain until Jesus comes or one of us goes home to be with the Lord. We know that it doesn't end there. We will see one another on the other side.

CONTENTS

Preface ix

CHAPTER 1   Sunday Morning 1

CHAPTER 2   The Question 7

CHAPTER 3   The Call... 12

CHAPTER 4   The Recovery 18

CHAPTER 5   Finally.. 23

CHAPTER 6   The Letdown 26

CHAPTER 7   The Anniversary 31

CHAPTER 8   Summertime 38

CHAPTER 9   The Cover-Up 42

CHAPTER 10 Sick and Tired....................................47

CHAPTER 11 The Arrest.. 53

CHAPTER 12 The Voice 60

CHAPTER 13 The Trial..69

CHAPTER 14 New Beginnings 84

PREFACE

Sonya Watkins is a fictional character with a very real situation. There are many Sonyas in the world who are in violent relationships, homes, and even marriages. Oftentimes these situations lead to the death of one or both parties in the relationship.

God gave me this book several years ago. I didn't think it would make a difference if I wrote a book or not, but the Holy Spirit wouldn't let me put this project down. I pray this book will help all the Sonyas around the world and help them realize that no matter how terrible your situation is and no matter how powerless you may feel, God can make a way out for you. Just as He did the children of Israel, He will do it for you in this present day.

Sonya Watkins is just the name that God gave me, but Sonya speaks for every man, woman, and child. God can deliver you from the hands of the enemy.

CHAPTER 1

SUNDAY MORNING

It was a cool fall day. The air was full of surprises, and the miracles of God were everywhere. I walked into Mount Carmel Baptist Church, the community church where I had been a member since I was a little girl. Nothing was wrong. All was going according to God's plan. The pastor's preaching was on point today. He was hitting the very channels of my heart. I could hear God saying to me, "Wisdom is the principle thing. Incline thine ear unto her, for she can save your soul."

As I inhaled the glory of God, I noticed him. Yes, *him*—that handsome young, tall, dark fellow worshipping the Lord in the second pew on the left side. I knew it! While I was supposed to be worshipping God, I was lusting after Mr. Tall, Dark, and Handsome. I should have been ashamed of myself, but he looked too good not to stare. I thought, *If this man looks my way, I am doomed.* The look on my face was pure lust, and I could feel it down in my soul. After the pastor preached, he always went into a worship service for the altar call. The songs were great, but I had my sights on something that I thought was greater.

As he bowed, I just imagined how life would be with Mr. Right. Several praise and worship songs proceeded before I realized that I had not taken my eyes off of this handsome specimen of a man. I heard absolutely nothing the pastor said during the benediction—not a single word. My mind was focused on the man on the other side of the room. He looked like everything I ever wanted in a man, especially when I saw this man worshipping the Lord.

Who didn't want a man who could bow down and worship the Lord and didn't care who was looking at him? He had tears in his eyes, wow! It looked as though he'd been sent from heaven. I had never seen this man before, but I hadn't been a faithful member of the church either. But the day I decided to be faithful and come to church on a regular basis in order to get myself together, this Adonis of a man showed up, and I noticed him.

After service as I was on my way to my car, I was in la-la land. All I could think of was this churchgoer who had taken my whole attention. I couldn't even remember where I had parked, but I kept walking because I had him on my mind.

That was when I heard, a deep voice behind me say, "Excuse me, sis."

I turned around, not thinking the voice was referring to me, and then I saw him. I thought, *Mr. Right! The man I was lusting all over during Sunday service!* My heart stopped. I didn't know what to say. Could this man really be talking to *me?* Wow! Yes, he was.

My soul leaped like John the Baptist in Elizabeth's belly when she saw her cousin Mary, the mother of Jesus. While I was going through all my emotions, he caught up with me, and he asked, "Excuse me, sis. Can I get a lift?"

I thought, *Out of all the fine women in Mount Carmel Baptist Church, this negro asks me for a ride.*

When I came to my senses, he was standing there with his hand extended. "I am so sorry. My name is Jake. My car just stalled."

He kept reaching out his hand. All the while I was standing there like a deer caught in headlights. I almost didn't accept his handshake.

"Well, ma'am, can I—"

After I came back down to earth and closed my mouth, I responded, "Oh yes, of course. I'm sorry. I am just not focused."

I shook his hand continually.

I knew it was the Lord. I just knew it.

We walked down the parking lot together, and all I could picture in my head was how I loved Jesus for sending me Mr. Right. On our way to the car, I could feel the haters looking at me like "Why is he walking with her?" or "I would have given him a ride." Maybe it was all in my head. All I knew was I was with the finest man of all times and he was getting in my car. Thank God I followed my mother's advice to always keep my car clean.

We had a really nice talk on the way to my car, or at least he answered all my questions. It was almost as if I was drilling him, and he knew it. He never evaded any of my questions, although I didn't go too deep. After all, it was our first date!

We finally arrived at my car. I'd had to park in the back of the parking lot because I was that member who got to church right before praise and worship.

Once at my car, he opened my door for me, even though I was the driver. I thought, *How nice. A handsome, saved man who's a gentleman.*

Even the ride to his house was very intriguing. He seemed to be a pleasant, laid-back kind of man. I really felt in my spirit that he was the one.

As we arrived at his neighborhood, it was nothing like I had expected. I thought he would have lived in a posh area. It wasn't bad. It just was not what I had expected because he was so nicely dressed and his car was a BMW. It was older but well kept. My expectations were probably a little too high.

So I dropped him off to his house, and before we parted ways, he asked, "Do you think my car will be okay in the parking lot?"

"Of course!" I said. "It's on God's property."

We both chuckled.

I rolled up my window as he walked away. We didn't exchange numbers, but I knew I would see him again. He was a churchgoing man.

Of course, I couldn't wait to get on the phone with my friends and tell them about what had happened. I couldn't get off his block quick enough before I called my girls on a three-way call. I was never a dater. I wasn't the best-looking cookie in the jar, so I was never really on anyone's hit list. Even in high school, no one asked me to prom, so I went alone. Well, that was neither here nor there. I'd just had a conversation with the finest man known to humankind. Well, at least in the church that I attended.

For several weeks I longed to go to church, not for the Word but for him, Mr. Right. His name was Jake. I knew he only needed a ride that day, but I saw more for us in the future. I envisioned him sweeping me off my feet and making me feel like *a natural woman*. (I thought that in my Aretha Franklin voice.) I would see Jake sitting in church across from me in his same row of pews, and I would peek over at him, giving him that tiny wave so that no one would see. You know church folks are nosy as heck. I'd been going to the same church since I was a little girl, and everyone knew my family. Momma didn't come anymore, and my baby sis took care of Momma because I worked a lot. So I was the only one who regularly attended Sunday services.

It'd been a while since I had dropped off Jake, and from the looks of things, he really didn't seem interested in me. He would give me his usual wave hello and smile with those pretty white teeth and then bring his focus back to what the pastor was saying. I got frustrated because I thought something was going to come out of our first date—that walk to the car. So I had to turn to my handy-dandy besties, and of course, my homegirls would give me tips on how I could get him to notice me more. The training was intense. I had to change my hair and makeup, and they even picked me out some really nice outfits every Sunday. But all I got was that smile and a tiny wave back. I tried eyelashes, lipsticks, lace fronts, half wigs, long weaves, short weaves. You name it, and I tried it. I figured I just happened to be the one to give him a ride when he needed one and nothing more.

CHAPTER 2

THE QUESTION

As time went by, I began to think that it was just a walk to the car and that I shouldn't get my hopes up high. Well, that was until Mr. Jake asked me on a date. I was on my way to my car once again, and I heard a voice. This time I knew who it was, so I turned around, ready.

"Hello, sis!" he said.

"Why, hello, Jake! What have I done to deserve such an honor?" I asked with extreme sarcasm.

"Well, first of all, my name is not Jake. It's Kevin. Kevin D. Watkins," he said with great confidence.

"Well, where did Jake come from?" I asked as I swung my hair around, thinking, *What is up with this guy with all these aliases?*

"That's just the name I use until I know I can trust someone."

"Oh, so you lie!" I blurted out, my one eyebrow raised.

Chuckling, Kevin looked at me and said, "I noticed you were looking really nice in church today."

"Thank you," I replied, thinking that my homies were right. I was feeling myself, and I was looking nice. But he was now noticing it.

He continued, "You didn't seem like all the other women I have met in the past. You didn't try to hound me down when you took me home that day. So that made me think you were a nice person, and I would like to know—" He paused then.

I thought to myself, *If this dude does not spit out of his mouth that he heard from the Lord and we are getting married, I am going to scream. Just kidding. Well, not really!* All I could say was, "Will you just spit it out?"

"Okay, okay," he said. "Will you have dinner with me?"

I said, "Yes, I will. I would love to have dinner with you."

He replied, "Great!" He walked away, and I got in my car just as excited as the first day I had taken him home.

On the way home, I realized that I didn't have his number and he didn't have mine, but I was still so excited that I couldn't contain myself. I thought about what to wear, how to act, and when my last date was. Actually, I had never been on a date. I was twenty-eight and had never been on a date. What was I doing all my life? I was just never that attractive to the opposite sex.

I didn't know when or how we were going to hook up, considering we hadn't exchanged numbers. I thought I could just go to his house. After all, I remembered where I had dropped him off. *Nah!* I thought that would make me seem thirsty. Well, some time passed since he'd asked the question, and I didn't even see Kevin in church for a few Sundays. I wondered if my mind was playing tricks on me. *Did he even ask me? Better yet, did I even see him?* Some might have thought that this behavior was a red flag, but it didn't matter to me. I was just happy a handsome man was even remotely attracted to me and willing to be seen in public with me on his shoulder.

It was good to have people I could trust to talk about my problems. I always took my friends' advice. After all, they had given me the great advice to give myself a makeover, which had worked just fine. That was how I had gotten asked on a date. My friends were awesome, but my main girl was Baby Sis. I didn't get much time with her because of my work schedule, and with her taking care of Momma, our time was limited. My baby sister was amazing. I had several conversations with Baby Sis, and she would tell me how I needed to just wait. She said, "He'll find a way to get to you if he is really interested."

Baby Sis always had men after her. Sometimes she made me feel like I was Celie and she was Nettie from *The Color Purple.* Baby Sis was the talk of the town when it came to Momma's girls. I looked like my daddy. I didn't get the looks that Baby Sis and even Momma got when they went out on the town. The town knew who we were, and every time I was alone and got some looks from the guys, they would ask that famous question with nasty grins on their faces: "How's that sister of yours?"

As time passed, Kevin frustrated me, and we weren't even dating. It appeared to me that I was on an up-and-down roller coaster with him since the day I had dropped him off. The fact that I hadn't seen him in church really made me angry because I didn't have any way of reaching him. Every church service became more and more disappointing. I would come in and look for Kevin where he usually sat, but he was never there. I thought, *I'm not sure how this dating thing is supposed to go, but if this is the way it is, I'm not sure I am going to like it.*

I knew Kevin was setting off red flags all around him, but I still believed this was God's plan and it was going to turn out well. I would keep looking for Kevin in church, but to no avail. I kept listening to Baby Sis's advice, and I always kept myself looking good just in case I ran into Mr. Right on any given Sunday. I even prayed to God and thanked him for my future husband. I thought I was so close to love, and it felt like the rug had been snatched out from under my feet. Even when the days seemed hopeless, I still kept my faith in God that I would see Kevin.

As the time passed without a call or a visit in church, I suddenly got this feeling like I wanted to put my head in the sand and keep it there. I felt like such an idiot. I always set myself up for a complete letdown. I decided to pay attention to the Word of God now. It had been so long since I had come to church for the Lord's message. God was my priority since I no longer had any more distractions. I gave up on the thought of ever seeing Mr. Right again, and as a result, God and I began to get acquainted again.

CHAPTER 3

THE CALL

As the days turned into weeks, I only wanted Wednesday or Sunday to come so that I can get the Word and continue my life. Yes, I had gotten so much better. I was even going to midweek services. It had been three months, and I had not seen him in church that whole time. My hopes totally dwindled, and I felt as though the whole date thing had just been the devil playing tricks on me. Or maybe Kevin was just being nice because I had dropped him off at home. I got back into the Word of God, and I could see things going well in my job and in my finances. I would get together with a couple friends so that we could have girls' nights out a few times during the month, and we even planned some trips.

Getting rid of the distractions in my life made a world of difference. I even found time to visit Momma and Baby Sis. I just wanted to check on them because Momma's health was deteriorating, but Baby Sis still managed to care for her and work a full-time job. Our time together was so special, and we made the best of it.

I really loved Sunday services, but boy, when it was over, I felt like I had worked a double shift at the job. As a result, Sundays were my nap days. After weeks of not seeing Mr. Right and giving up hope, my emotions were finally at ease, and I enjoyed me all over again— until around three in the afternoon when my phone rang. Reluctantly, I answered it. Normally, I didn't answer my house phone. It was mostly telemarketers who called the house. It stopped ringing, but then it began to ring again, so I thought it might be important. "Hello?" I said. I was prepared to hang up the phone if it was indeed a telemarketer.

"I know you thought I had flown the coop." I held the phone away from my face because I didn't know the voice. "Sony?" the voice said.

"Yes, it's me," I answered, still in bewilderment.

"It's me, Jake … uh, Kevin."

"Oh yes, yeah. Oh, I'm sorry." I thought to myself, *It's him!*

He began by saying, "I just want to apologize for not getting back with you. I had a really busy week."

"You mean months and weeks?" I interrupted him with caution, but I still wanted him to know I was a little upset.

"Yes, I know you must think I'm a real jerk."

"No, I was just wondering what happened to you because we never exchanged numbers. Wait a minute. How did you get my number?" I blurted out.

"Well, I have friends in very high places."

"Oh, really?" I said, all the while thinking that this guy was a stalker.

"I'm talking to you, right?" he said.

"Well, yes, but on my house phone," I answered. "Anyhoo, Mr. Kevin, how are you?"

"You can save all those questions for our date," he said abruptly. I could have fallen out of my skin when he said that.

"Well, all righty then. I guess I should be asking when and where," I said.

"No, I'll be there to pick you up in an hour."

"Wait! What? Hello? Hello?" He had hung up. I thought, *Did this negro just hang up on me?*

All mayhem happened in my head as I was trying to get dressed and ready. This man was taking me out. *Wait until I tell my girls and Baby Sis*, I thought. *What do I do? How do I act?* This was so intense. Finally, Mr. Right Dee Luv—that was what I started calling him—was taking me out. I had refreshed so many times when the doorbell rang. I was still look-ing in the mirror, trying to put the finishing touches to my look. "Just a minute," I yelled. As I went to the door, still fixing my hair, I opened it to find a tall, handsome, nice-smelling man. I couldn't even speak, my mouth just hung open.

"Well, are you going to speak?" he said, looking down at me.

When I came out of my initial shock, I said, "Yeah, yes." Then I stuttered and said, "Come, come in."

He just chuckled as I offered him a seat and ran to the bathroom to fix my hair, which was already fixed.

When I returned to the sitting room, Kevin, stood up in my living room and asked me, "Are you ready?"

I was as ready as I could be, so off we went. The drive was very intense. He smelled so good that I felt part of my womanhood stir. He took the edge off the intensity of the drive by striking up a conversation. Then we found ourselves reminiscing on our past. It turned out we had both grown up poor. It was so amazing we talked about PB&J and mayonnaise sandwiches. I didn't go too deep because I had just met him, but I had so many questions. I figured I'd keep them for later.

Finally, we arrived at Sambo's, the best restaurant in town for fine dining. I was in awe because I never thought I would be able to afford something like this. I tried not to seem so stunned because the desserts were seven dollars each and the entrées started at more than fifteen dollars. He seemed to be at ease with the atmosphere. Even though he had picked the place, I was a little concerned about the bill. I ordered very gingerly as I gazed over the menu. I heard him say, "Pretty lady, order whatever you want."

I almost lost it. "Even dessert?" I asked as I giggled.

"Yes, even dessert." We both chuckled. As the night progressed, I would catch him gazing at me with those light brown eyes that complemented his sandy complexion.

I could smell his sexy cologne from across the table. The way he chewed his food and wiped his mouth after every bite made me think sinful thoughts. We ordered cocktails, and of course, he ordered for me. I wasn't a big drinker, but he seemed to know exactly what to order. One might say that was another red flag. We enjoyed our meal, and the chocolate cake was so good. I really liked chocolate, and so did he. We shared the dessert because it was so big. I didn't want to eat it all by myself, but I didn't want to leave it either.

When the bill came, I was so confused because I didn't know what to do. I kept thinking, *Do I reach for the bill, or do I just let him pay it?* All sorts of bad thoughts ran through my mind. *If I don't try to help, maybe he won't invite me out again, or if I take the bill, maybe he will think I'm too strong. What to do?* My jaw was clinched. Sweat was running down my face, or at least that was what it felt like. With my lips tucked in, I reached for the bill. His hand touched mine, and he said, "Baby, your money is no good here." I relaxed my jaw and explained to him that I had never been on a date and that I really didn't know what to expect. He looked at me, and I melted when he said, "Your money is no good with me." I just knew right then he was the one.

When he took care of the bill, I felt like I really had found the right man for me. He was a protector and a provider. What more could a woman ask for from a man? The ride back was really fun. We shared our likes and dislikes, places we would like to visit, things we would like to see, and the people we wanted to go with. We created a bucket list. Some things were so far-fetched like a trip to the moon, but we both laughed at ourselves. We sang old songs that we had grown up on. We would keep switching stations so that we could catch a song we both knew. It was magical. Life was good, and it could not get any better.

Well, the time had come for us to part. We reached my apartment, and the night was over. I wondered whether he was going to try to kiss me or just going to drop me off like a friend. When he pulled up to my place. He reached over and kissed me on my forehead. Then he got out of the car, walked over to my door, and let me out. He walked me to my door and said, "Good night, pretty lady. I'll talk to you tomorrow."

"Good night, Kevin. I'll talk to you later." I closed the door and ran to the window just to watch him walk to his car. I knew I would have to repent just for the sinful thoughts I had then.

CHAPTER 4

THE RECOVERY

It took a few days to come down from the initial blast from the date, but I knew it was a pivotal point in my life. God was blessing me, and I just knew it. Days passed, and he had not called me back. Of course, I thought the worst. Maybe I was supposed to sleep with him after all the money he had spent, or maybe he found someone new. My mind went haywire. I ran to church just to see him, but he wasn't there. That should have been red flag number three. I couldn't imagine what had happened to Mr. Right. He wasn't at church, and he wasn't calling. I stopped listening to the Word of God again and focused on not seeing Kevin. I just kept wondering, *God, what happened? I was so close again, and the rug was just yanked out from under my feet.*

It had to be around midnight when the phone rang. I was so scared to answer the phone. I didn't want it to not be him. The phone kept ringing, so I finally answered it. "Hello!" I said in my sleepy voice.

"Sony? It's me, Kevin."

"Oh, hey, how have you been?" I was really playing it cool, but a part of me wanted to say, "Boy, have you lost your mind? Where in the hell have you been?" But of course, I waited to hear what he was going to say.

"Babe, I know I keep disappearing on you. I have a lot of things going on, and I don't want you to be caught up in my mess."

"Okay. No, no, it's okay, but you have to call or something because I get worried." Some would say that was red flag number four.

I began to tell him how I was so worried about him, and he interrupted me, "Well, if you were so worried, why didn't you call to check up on me?" After I got over the initial shock of that question, he interrupted my thoughts by saying, "Girl, I'm just joking." I suddenly released the gas that had bubbled up in my stomach. "What are you doing?" he asked.

"I'm … like in bed."

"Well, can I come over?" Fumbling over my words, I said yes. When I looked at the clock, I realized it was almost one o'clock in the morning. I thought about how unprepared I was for company. I could hear Momma saying, "Sony, always keep yourself and house visitor ready." I hurried to clean and also cook a meal in twenty minutes. It didn't dawn on me that he was coming at a very unusual hour. That was probably red flag number five. Of course, I didn't see it. Or rather I didn't want to see the flags.

When he arrived, he looked and smelled good as usual. I invited him in. He could clearly smell the ground beef in sauce simmering with garlic and oregano and the seasoned spaghetti noodles boiling. "Hello, Sonya. You look very pretty tonight."

I giggled. "You mean this morning?" We both chuckled. "I cooked you a little something just in case you were hungry." He planted a kiss on my lips that made every part of me stand at attention.

That moment I felt all that I would ever need was at my feet, and I didn't even realize that he wasn't kissing me anymore. He rubbed my chin and looked at me as if I was the only one who mattered in this world. From that moment on, everything went wrong. Momma always said, "Forbidden fruit always taste good." I couldn't remember whether I knew the Lord or not.

I knew I was going to be another church statistic the next morning. I had never been on a date before, but I wasn't a virgin. I had had some flings here and there. Nothing I would call a relationship. Kevin was the first to take me out before the sex. Normally, the guy and I would have sex and never get to the date part. Before I knew it, they would be gone. Mr. Right kissed my body in places I had forgotten about. My whole body tingled with a sensation that I have never felt before.

He took control of my body, and I let him. He was an excellent driver. I screamed several times in ecstasy as he moved my body into various positions. As he made circular motions between my thighs, God was the furthest thing from my mind. He drove me for so long that it was dawn when he finally ran out of gas. The morning finally came. I tried not to make unnecessary conversation. I just stared out the window, wondering how I had messed up such a good thing.

"Baby! Baby, you okay?" I heard him, but I was too embarrassed to turn around. I couldn't speak until he left the room. After I was sure he was gone, I ran to the kitchen only to find him sitting at the table. "I thought you would never wake up," he said. I kept my head down as I walked to the refrigerator.

"Well, I never had a night like that before," I said with all the shame in the world. He walked over to me and caressed me, and we made love again right there in the kitchen. I thought this session was never going to end. Kevin was a stallion, or maybe I just didn't have enough experience. I was never a heavy woman, but he just scooped me up and rammed my back against the refrigerator. He made deep wide circles inside me. My eyes rolled back in my head, and I just moaned for hours until he ran out of gas again.

This went on for six months. I knew it was wrong, but I didn't want to be right. I wanted this man at all costs. Given the way he made me feel, think, and love, I was willing to take all the risks. That might have been red flag number five or six. I had lost count of all the flags. I still didn't know his work status or anything about his personal background. I didn't see any clear signs about those, but if there were, I didn't want to see them.

The sex was wonderful. I had never been with a man who had made me feel this good in my whole entire life. The sex was out of this world. It happened two or three times every night. I lost so much weight I needed a new wardrobe. How could this man possess so much energy and keep a full-time job? He would come over every night. He knew my schedule. Many times he'd be right there when I got home. He would get out of his car when I was getting out of mine. There were so many red flags.

CHAPTER 5

FINALLY

Because of the sinful life I had fallen into, the outside fellowship and of course church came to a screeching halt. I rarely saw Baby Sis or Momma because Kevin practically moved in. He was there when I left and there when I came home. He would have dinner ready almost every day, and I really couldn't complain because at least he wasn't disappearing anymore. He was right where I wanted him—with me.

Yes, he practically moved in without asking me. I didn't even realize that we hadn't gone out or hung out with any of my friends for almost a year. When one of us girls got a man, we just let them be, and if it didn't last, we would be right there to help with them with their broken heart. Since this was my first rodeo, they didn't even try to bother me. They knew it was my first love, and just like me, they thought God had organized this.

We didn't do much outside of the bedroom for

almost six months. I would go to work and come home, and then we'd fornicate. After months of sinful bliss, he popped the question. One day I was cooking us some dinner, and out of the clear blue sky, he said, "Baby, let's get married."

Of course, I said yes without hesitation. I was already living in sin and not going to church, and I thought marriage would fix my mess. I was so elated that I burned the spaghetti. I was distracted because we went right to the bedroom before dinner was done.

I must have given Kevin the best I had, as he kept asking, "Baby, what got into you?"

I just chuckled because I was so excited. "You, I guess," I replied, and we both laughed. That was when we realized that the stench was not our intense love-making lust but spaghetti sauce burning to the pan.

We jumped up as fast as we could, falling over the sheets as we tried to keep ourselves covered. We laughed at ourselves as we ate spaghetti and burnt sauce. "Baby, this is so good!" he said, even though I could see the disgust on his face.

"Stop lying!" I replied. I knew he was just kidding around by the look on his face every time he took a bite.

Dinner didn't end well, so we got some takeout to eat that night. Surprisingly, Kevin said, "Hey, babe, you mind getting this? I haven't gotten paid yet."

"Yeah, sure. I don't mind," I said. At the time I

didn't think that this was the beginning of me paying for everything.

I didn't see the signs. Well, I didn't want to see the signs. Kevin would have food on the table almost every night that he cooked. I never saw him leave for work. He'd be there when I left and when I came home. He wasn't paying any bills, and I didn't force him to pay because it was my place. Plus I didn't want anything to mess up this so-called good thing.

Well, we got married by the justice of the peace. I thought it was the best thing that had ever happened to me, but nobody knew it. We did things so abruptly. Baby Sis found out over the phone, and my girls just gave up on me and just said, "Well, Sonya is out the group." I still had this feeling like I had messed up more than I thought I had. Happiness was in front of me, and all I wanted to do was be happy. Our lovemaking was no longer fornicating, and that was the only thing I needed to be right. I thought everything else would fall right into place.

CHAPTER 6

THE LETDOWN

Out of all the marital bliss and the many meals I ended up paying for when Kevin didn't feel like cooking, I began to wonder about his employment, especially since he never spoke of his job. I came to find out that Kevin was a handyman that nobody found handy. He was the type of man who looked like he had a good job but couldn't actually keep a job to save his life. He'd have some money sometimes, but that never lasted. He acted like every company that let him go was delusional about his worth and that they didn't know what kind of employee they were letting go. He thought he was the best thing since sliced bread.

As the months went by, I began to support him after every layoff, every financial dilemma, and every get-rich-quick scheme. As our debt increased, Mr. Right suddenly became Mr. Wrong. *What am I supposed to do?* I thought. Oh well, I made this bed, and now I had to lie in it. I was working hard and getting a promotion, and of course, I had enough money to pay for my car, which he drove more than me. He felt I should be taken to work and picked up. *Really!* I thought. *Maybe it's because your car has seen better days and today is not one of them.*

Of course, I didn't say that, but I felt like it. I paid all the bills and put food on the table and gas in my car. I paid for it all. I would read captions on the web about how women should not struggle if there were men in their lives. I didn't think it applied to me because I wasn't struggling—at least not at this point.

We didn't go out as a couple either. In fact, Sambo's was our only date. We spent most of our time at home in bed, at the table, or in the living room and eating what I cooked or bought when I didn't feel like cooking. We would talk less and less, but he would make suggestions all the time. He would blurt out, "Hey, baby," and I always answered, "Yeah," knowing it would be something that I was going to have to fund. "Why don't we put our money together? You know like share a bank account."

"Okay," I said like a dummy. I thought, *What money? You don't pay a damn thing, and you don't have any money.*

He would continue, "I mean, that's only right. We are married, and couples should share accounts."

I would answer, "Yes, honey, you're right."

The whole time I was sitting and thinking, *How in the hell does he believe that banking together is right? It's right to go to church together, but we haven't been to church since we had sex.*

Like a dummy, I went to the bank and put his name on my account. Once the transaction was completed, he lit up like a light bulb. "Baby, that's great! God can pour into our lives because we are together now."

Reluctantly, I replied, "Yes, I believe that."

"Really, Sony?"

But I didn't believe that. For that matter, we never stopped at his bank to put my name on his accounts. I was getting pissed now.

"Baby!" I said softly, holding in my frustrations. "Do you have a bank account?"

"Why would you ask me a thing like that?" he asked me with a smile.

"Well, you said—"

"I know what I said. You have everything I own, Sony."

"I know, but I should be on yours too, shouldn't I?"

"Sony, listen. I don't have a bank account because my crazy ex-girlfriend made some fraudulent trans-actions on my bank accounts, so I had to close them, baby! Listen, I don't want nothing from you, just your love."

"But why am I paying all the bills?" I asked in my

loving but frustrated voice. For a minute I thought I had come across a rattlesnake until he gripped the steering wheel and calmed down.

"I don't like having to tell you this, but I guess you need to know. After my ex took all my money and my investments, I had to start rebuilding my credit and everything." I felt a little better knowing a little about what I thought was the truth, so I kept quiet and allowed him to explain. "My plans are to buy you a house and a new car, baby! I just need you to just hold on. I am going to take the load off of you in a little bit." He reached over and held my hand.

"Okay," I said. I felt so small. "I'm so sorry."

"No, baby, please don't be. I know I am supposed to be the provider and the shot caller. Just give me a minute."

"I will, honey. I'm so sorry. Why did she do you like that?" I asked.

"Listen. I … I really don't want to talk about that bi— I just don't want to talk about it. Let me recover and do right by you, okay?"

I replied, "Okay. I'm sorry."

"And stop apologizing. You did nothing wrong."

We drove home in silence. Neither Kevin nor I had much to say. Since Kevin had access to my account, there was always something wrong with the money. Bills were not getting paid on time because he was taking money out and wasn't telling me. Consequently, when I went to pay the bills, I would have insufficient funds. When I would question him about it, he always went off the handle like I had done something wrong, or he'd claim he didn't know what happened. Keep in mind that he still wasn't contributing to the bank account. He would pay one thing and expect me to swing on the chandelier with excitement, and when I didn't, he would cop an attitude as though I was ungrateful. I would think, *How can I be grateful when I pay everything and you pay one water bill for twenty-five dollars after I paid seventeen water bills? Sorry but not sorry. I'm not excited.* But of course, I couldn't tell that wonderful work of art that I was not impressed with him.

CHAPTER 7

THE ANNIVERSARY

Of course, our second anniversary was grand like everything he did for me that I paid for. Even though we never did anything during the year, he made sure that we had a lavish anniversary. Where did we get the money from? That answer was a no-brainer. It came from all the other bills we didn't pay during the year, but this year was different. I decided to set the record straight.

As soon as I walked in the door from work, I began taking off my coat. I was fed up trying to please this man by being quiet. I had had enough. I said, "Tonight we are going over the bills to see where we can fix this mess we are in." What did I say that for? He went ballistic, and all hell broke loose. I went from the love of his life to the bitch who never supported him.

All I could do was sit still in my chair, stunned by what had just transpired. My whole life flashed before me as tears rolled down my cheeks. I thought about how I had allowed my life to be shattered by a man who was in and out of employment and now verbally abusive. Was I wrong for feeling like we were spiraling downhill financially? We were down to one car, and the way things looked, it seemed that we might have to start taking public transportation. Yes, I was behind on my car payment. Plus the brakes and tires needed work. Kevin really pushed the car to the limit after he dropped me off at work.

The next day I was totally unsure about the man I was waking up next to, so I just laid there and prayed. Saturdays were usually just like any other day, but on this day Kevin left early and stayed out all day. I made sure that the house was clean and that dinner was on the table. I wanted to avoid any confrontation or inviting the man I had met yesterday. I still didn't know who that man was.

After six in the evening, I began to think the worst. Maybe he had felt so bad that he killed himself, or maybe he had gotten into a car accident. Only the worst came to my mind. At eleven o'clock in the evening, I just couldn't bare it. Now that we no longer have cell phones, so there was no way to contact him.

At one o'clock in the morning, I heard the keys in the lock, and I jumped up as soon as he walked in. Out of concern, I asked, "Where have you been?" Oh no, I had invited that vicious man to come back.

"Bitch, don't you ever ask me where the fuck I've been. Get in the room, and take your clothes off."

I stood there like a dear caught in headlights. In my mind, I kept saying, "What just happened?" I felt like Celie from *The Color Purple* when she said Mr. just used the bathroom on her. I felt like I had cheated on my husband. I was sleeping with someone I did not know.

He pounded on me like I was a whore, and when he finished, he rolled over, wiped his dick off with the sheets, and went to sleep. I felt like I was sleeping with the enemy. Days turned into weeks, and weeks turned into months of physical and verbal abuse. I couldn't tell anyone because I could hear them say, "I knew it was too soon," or, "You should have waited." What was I supposed to do? I couldn't stay in sin. I had to do the right thing by God. After a life-changing experience as mine, someone saying, "I told you so," is not exactly comforting.

My world had turned into hell overnight. Of course, I knew it was changing, but the extremity was a bit difficult. After months of missing payments on my car, the bank finally repossessed it. That wasn't too bad. It was on its last leg anyway, and I would have had two more years of payments. So I started using public transportation. I worked deep into the city, so the subway was the best way to get to and from work. I thought some days were the worst days of my life. Then one day a male coworker gave me a lift home since I had to stay late to complete a task.

Of course, when I got home, Kevin was there. As soon as I got into the house, I felt a large hand around my throat, and I was called everything but a child of God. I felt like my life had been cracked open as he pressed a steel toe boot on my uterus. I remember thinking, *Why in the world would someone have steel toe construction boots but no job?*

The room began to spin, and I just zoned out as I watched his huge shadow over me pounding me with his boots. I went numb, but I could feel the pressure of his boot pounding my pelvic area. Finally, when the beating was over, all I could do was just lie there. I could not move my legs, and I felt something warm and wet between my legs. I wanted to get up so that I could clean myself up and go to bed; however, the room got really blurry, and I couldn't seem to keep my eyes open.

When I came to my senses, I was in the hospital. I knew exactly what had happened, but I didn't remember going to the hospital. I turned my head, and I could see him like a demon waiting to attack. The doctor came in the room and began to explain to me that my uterus was ruptured beyond repair and that I needed an emergency hysterectomy to save my life. The tears burned my eyes. I tried desperately to repress my emotions. I was afraid.

Kevin just stood there. The more the doctor explained to him how serious my injury was, the angrier he got. I got confused when the doctor started explaining to him how the car accident could have killed me and how it was an act of God that the engine didn't crush my legs. All I could do was lie there and think to myself, *How can I be in a car accident when I don't have a car? Who was the driver? Where's the police report?* I couldn't muster the energy to argue.

I wanted to choke that young doctor for not asking the pertinent questions. *It's him!* I thought. *He tried to kill me!* I just laid there as a tear rolled down my cheek. I watched the doctor leave the room. Kevin was alone with me now, and he stood over me like a demon. "So you ain't gonna be able to bear me no children? You sure are fucked up now, ain't you? Ain't you?" He couldn't hurt me any more than I already was. I couldn't even cry anymore. I was dead inside. No words could articulate the emotional pain I was feeling. I had to stay a week in the hospital to ensure I healed properly from the hysterectomy. Kevin came a few times, but he never stayed long. During every visit he would express his anger, and then he would make up some excuse to leave.

The horrific time had come. I was released to go home. I kept trying to play it safe. I couldn't walk, laugh, cough, or cry, and I was scared to ask for help.

To my surprise, Kevin helped me into the wheelchair and pushed me. He even borrowed the neighbor's car to pick me up from the hospital. When we arrived home, I saw he had cooked some food and had cleaned the house. For a moment, I thought I had really been in a car accident and had dreamed the whole horror story. "Kevin!" someone said. Then a beautiful woman came out of our bedchambers.

"Hey, thanks, Sis, for helping me with dinner and cleaning up," he said to the beautiful lady.

"Oh, no problem. It's good to have you home, Mrs. Watkins. I guess I'll be going then." As she left the house, I had so many questions, but I dared not ask her. To my surprise, he volunteered information about her. It turned out that she was one of the members of the church—yes, the same church we hadn't been to in years. She'd heard about my car accident and had come over to help. I thought to myself, *Really? She came to help? No one came to check on our salvation, but she came to clean up and feed me after an accident I didn't have?* Well, I knew if I contested his story, my breasts would be the next body part he'd attack, and then I'd no longer be a woman.

I only could eat as much as the pain would allow, but the sister sure could cook. The food was really good. She must be from the South. It took eight weeks before I could walk right. By that time, I had lost my job. The doctor explained that since the trauma was so significant, it would take my body longer to heal. While I was unemployed, Kevin was still working. Or at least the bills were getting paid somehow.

I knew I had to stick with the car accident story, or I would be done for. But of all lies, how could anyone believe I was in a car accident when I had no car? I couldn't tell Baby Sis or Momma because I didn't want them to contend with Kevin either.

CHAPTER 8

SUMMERTIME

Summer came again, and everyone was out playing and enjoying life. I decided to show my face in public again. For years I had not seen my friends or family members. I'd just been cooped up in the house. Today I decided to go out and get some fresh air. Surprisingly, many people approached me and said, "Good to see you're doing better," and, "You look so good since that car accident." Many of my neighbors were outside enjoying the summer breeze. I decided to spend a few moments with them.

We laughed and talked until the sun went down. I totally forgot I had a husband to cook for. I looked up and saw Kevin walking down the street. I knew he was angry when he saw me. He looked like a raging bull. He greeted everyone and looked at me as if I needed to get up and follow him into the house. Of course, I explained how sorry I was for letting the time get away from me and not preparing supper.

When he sat down, he only gave me five minutes to make him a hot meal. Of course, I failed, and the beatings began again. This time they didn't stop. Day in and day out, he would beat me. I was so sore from the beatings I had received the day before that I was not able to move. Kevin was smart though. After sending me to the hospital before, he knew he could only punch my body and choke me. He knew not to hurt me enough to hospitalize me. He would beat me just enough to cause bruises. Many times I was beaten because I was too sore to cook, and he would just snap. I felt like I was in a constant cycle of abuse, and every day he would just keep beating me. I got into the habit of bracing myself for impact.

I would look in the mirror and notice that the once not so attractive young lady was now very ugly. I couldn't see a speckle of beauty in this face. I managed to keep my front teeth, but Kevin had punched out the ones on the side of my mouth. At the age of thirty-two, I just cried because I looked like a hard fifty-year-old. Asking God for help was out of the question because I was a sinner. At least that was what I was told. But I was so tired of getting beaten and remaining silent. I was sick and tired of being sick and tired. I looked so beat down and tired. I was alienated from my friends, family, and anyone who could ask me what was going on.

It would appear to anyone that I'd had enough, but

I stuck in there. The beatings eased up though. I wasn't able to handle too many more without a trip to the emergency room. Kevin had an understanding about one thing. Too many trips to the hospital would not be good for him. I couldn't go back to work either because someone would catch on that I was being beaten to a pulp. The emotional roller coaster never ceased, and my tolerance grew thin. While Kevin was at work, I began talking to my sister. Baby Sis was young, beautiful, and energetic. She would visit me, and I would tell her that I had never really recovered from the car accident—the one I never had—and that the pain medication was keeping me under the weather in actuality, I was getting my ass kicked day in and day out.

When Baby Sis said she was getting married, I thought to myself, *I hope he's nothing like Kevin.* But David seemed like a sweetheart with the cute smile of a little boy. David was a hard worker, and nothing seemed to bother him much. He was laid-back and easygoing. Baby Sis didn't ask much of me when it came to planning her wedding. She figured I wasn't really able to help or serve in the wedding because of the accident.

Any visit from Baby Sis was good. We laughed, talked, and reminisced about our childhood. She would come over as often as she could, and we'd giggle. Then I would rush her off before Kevin came home. The last thing I needed was Kevin seeing Baby Sis coming over and thinking that I was involving her in our mess. I am just not sure what would happen if they would meet in person. Baby Sis was very protective of me, and if she sensed that Kevin was in any way, shape, or form abusive, she would have his head on a platter. I couldn't risk getting her involved in this hellish mess. After all, she needed to be available for Momma and her husband.

CHAPTER 9

THE COVER-UP

Baby Sis had become a frequent visitor after she and David tied the knot. She cut down on her hours at work, and she had more time to spend with me and Momma. The wedding was beautiful. My sister looked like an angel. Tears of joy ran down my face when I saw her floating down the aisle. Oh, how I wished I had a wedding. I hadn't seen my folks in years. Although Momma suffered from mild dementia, she seemed to be fine. She even recognized me.

I knew I didn't look good, and my legs were often in pain. In fact, I would drag whatever leg hurt the most. However, no one dared to tell me I looked anything but good. At the wedding he was extra caring, telling everyone that I was still recovering from the car accident I had never had. I just hung my head down low as I heard him say, "I was so scared. I thought my baby was going to die. The doctors said if she would have gotten hit a little bit harder, she would have been paralyzed." My stomach turned every time I heard him recite his theatrics.

I just thought to myself, Yeah, if you would have kept on stomping me in my stomach, I would be dead, but of course, I just didn't say anything.

But there were some people who stared Kevin down because no one really knew him and we had just gotten married so abruptly. Then it seemed that we disappeared off the face of the earth. My girls or the people who used to be my girls were there, and of course, they pulled me to the side. One of them said, "Girl, that is a fine piece of artwork! Is that why you kept him locked up?" I just smirked to keep from blurting out, "He's trying to kill me! Help!"

I just said, "Yes, he is."

"I mean, he is really taking care of you after the car accident."

All agreed that he was a good man, but I just nodded my head and said, "Yeah, he does his best."

"Girl, a man that tall. I know the sex is off the chain."

"Yeah! Tell us," another one said.

I could have fainted. Kevin had not touched me in a loving way in such a long time that I couldn't remember what it was like to actually make love to my husband. So I just shook my head. "Well, you know I'm not one to kiss and tell," I said with a chuckle.

"Girl, you still silly," one of the girls said.

"We miss you, and when you get well, we have to have a girls' night out," another said.

Right before I agreed, Kevin showed up. "Sony, let's get ready to go."

"Okay. Girls, look, I gotta go, but I love y'all."

We hugged and kissed, and I knew that it would be a while before I saw my friends again. It was good while it lasted though.

One day Baby Sis came by to visit. She had this look about her. It seemed like the look Momma had when God gave her a word. She sat down at the kitchen table and didn't hesitate to make herself something to drink, and when she sat down, she looked me flat in the eyes and asked, "How are you?"

Of course I said I was fine.

Her reply was like a sucker punch in the face. "I can't tell. You look like hell."

I could have fallen out of my skin twice. I stuttered and said, "You know I still haven't fully recovered from the accident." Boy did I feel like a total ass saying the same thing Kevin said. I knew damn well I wasn't in a car accident. I didn't even own a car anymore.

I learned that Kevin had actually decided to use the car as collateral before we lost it. Yes, I did a title loan when Kevin wasn't working because he spent all the money and didn't care how the bills are paid. When I wasn't able to catch up, the bank repossessed the car. Baby Sis was not one to pry. If you gave her an answer, she took what you gave her, and that was it. I got up to go to the bathroom, and before I could get far, I broke down in tears like a baby. I thought, *How could I be so stupid?* My mind raced. I wondered if she could tell I was lying. Oh, if Momma was in her right mind, she would have spotted that lie and told me what the truth was. I wasn't as old as I looked, but I looked so old that a person might think I was a SSI recipient. She was right. I did look bad, but there was nothing I could do about it.

Baby Sis's visits became less frequent since David and Momma required her attention. My depression had gotten so bad that I wanted to kill myself. The physical abuse had lessened, but somehow, he'd find another way to tear me apart. The verbal and mental abuse was more than anyone could handle. Kevin was so disrespectful too. He would watch pornography while I was sitting in the same room and begin to masturbate. He would tell me that the reason that he had to watch porn and fantasize about other women was because I had let myself go so bad that he could not stand to make love to an old hag.

I just looked into the air and thought about how the feeling was mutual. I did not miss him or his touch. However, I did receive his touch but not in the way I wanted. In fact, it had been years since I had the urge to be sexual with a man. I was in such a dark place, I would sleep until it was time to get up and cook Kevin some dinner. I woke up only to dream about going back to sleep. The days became a blur. I didn't care to know what day it was. I just needed the time.

I knew it couldn't and wouldn't get any better. I was just going on day by day, second by second, hoping one day I just wouldn't wake up. Every day my hopes would diminish. Some might say I was angry at God, but really, I was angry at myself. After all, I did this to myself by falling into sin and trying to fix it myself by getting married to a man I hardly knew. I didn't dare be angry at God.

CHAPTER 10

SICK AND TIRED

One Friday I got up to cook Kevin some dinner. I went to sit down for a minute only to fall back to sleep. I woke up Saturday morning around seven o'clock only to find that Kevin had not come home. His plate had been sitting on the table the whole night. Before I could get the dishes off the table, he walked in as he was talking to someone. "Okay, baby, I'll see you later," he said as he hurried in the door. I saw her, and she saw me just before he pushed her out the door and closed it in her face. I could hear her saying, "I didn't know your mother was home."

I could hear her giggling as she walked away from the door. I felt like I was sick. I ran to the bathroom to vomit. He never said a word about her. Nor did he ask me was I okay. "Did you cook?" he asked.

"I had to throw it away. It sat on the table all night," I replied.

"Bitch! Do I look like I have money growing out

of my ass?" He began to rant and rave. I just stopped. I looked at him as if to say, "Please not today. I can't do this today. Since I didn't answer him, he began to scream and holler, but I just didn't have any more defenses. I could not even cry. I just walked away, or rather I hobbled away. My pelvic area often felt stiff, and my joints would become inflamed because of my lack of mobility. Surprisingly, he didn't hit me today. I felt some relief and went back to bed. All I did was sleep and get up and cook for Kevin.

Even though he didn't hit me that day, he continued the next. He ranted and raved for two days straight, and all I could do was sit there. I couldn't even defend myself when he slapped me and spit in my face. He'd hit me so hard sometimes that I'd see stars like cartoon characters would.

My world seemed to shift every time he would land a hit. Sometimes it would feel like I was taking quantum leaps from planets. He'd slap me on one side, and when I'd come to, I'd see him looking at another part of the house and wondering when the last time I had dusted that shelf.

One day I got up and went for a walk, I needed to walk because my bones were stiff. It felt so good to get out and see what the world had to offer. Smelling the fresh air and seeing things other than undusted shelves and four walls that really needed a paint job. And I wanted to get away from abuse. I ended up walking for two days in a row. I went to stores, looked around, and saw many nice things that I'd love to have. Before I met Kevin, I always treated myself. At least once a month, I had to treat myself to an article of clothing or a pair of shoes.

I walked into a store that women normally wouldn't go into, but I wanted to take a look inside. I went through every aisle without even thinking about the time. I had decided I was going to purchase something that I had been eying for a really long time. I didn't have any money, so I when I saw it, my hopes were shattered. I thought to myself, *How am I going to purchase this when I don't have any money?* When I left the store, the wheels in my brain started turning. I couldn't even sleep that night.

After I cooked Kevin dinner, but he didn't come home to eat again. Then a light bulb went off in my head. I called Baby Sis and told her I wanted to purchase something for myself. She was elated, and without hesitation, she brought me the money. The next day I got up and ran back to the store and bought the item! My life was moving in the right direction. At least that was how I felt. I hadn't been able to buy myself anything in years.

I knew Kevin could never find out, so I hid the item in the backyard. Baby Sis knew I wasn't going to pay her back because I hadn't worked in years. Kevin would never find out about my purchase.

In her excitement Baby Sis asked what I had purchased. She was so eager to know what I had bought, but of course, I didn't want her to slip up and tell Kevin if they ever crossed paths. I told her it was best for all of us that we keep it secret. Baby Sis trusted me, and she knew that I had my reasons, so she just left it alone.

Well, I was at peace with my gift to myself, a nice shiny axe. I felt the anticipation of using it too. The moment was just a whisper away. I knew when I would have a good reason when I used my gift. The days were longer. The nights were lonely, and when Kevin would come home smelling like women, he would let me know how he had to do what he had to do because of what I let happened to myself. I felt like I had been bamboozled. *I didn't do this to myself,* I thought. *This was done to me.*

Rage stirred inside of me. I never asked him to stomp on me until my uterus was shattered. I never asked him to punch me until he knocked out my teeth.

Kevin had no idea what was coming his way, but I kept my cool. He pursued many women and disrespected me at every turn. It seemed my personal business was everywhere. Whenever I would walk around just to clear my head, I could stroll into the store around the corner of the block and overhear little stories about

Kevin and some of the women down the street. I even overheard some stories that he had an STD. How could I know if it was true? He hadn't touched me in years. It was like I was in *The Twilight Zone*. All the voices and murmurings filled my mind for days on end.

I continued to walk and hear the stories. Sometimes I would ask questions just to get all the filthy details. People I had never met were so eager to tell me about my sorry-ass husband. I was so depressed. Nights were the worst for me. The torment was intense. I started hearing voices during the night. One evening I heard it loud and clear when it said, "It is time!"

I couldn't quite make out whose voice it was, but I knew in my heart it was time to make a move. It was about five thirty in the morning. The smell of alcohol filled the room, and Kevin was sound asleep. I could smell the other woman's body on his face. It was so strong that it seemed as if she was sleeping in the bed with us. He would always come home when I was sleep, but tonight I woke up after he had lain down. At this time I knew I had to follow my heart. I went into the backyard to get my gift. I put my gloves on and bought my new gift into the house.

The sun had not come up yet, but I could see him clearly in the bed. I raised my gift over my head and then plunged it forcibly into his chest. As I released the gift, his eyes popped open in a split second. The gift landed with so much force that I heard his sternum crack and blood splashed everywhere. I just couldn't stop there. I kept landing blows with precision over and over until Kevin looked like ground beef. Then I laid my gift right beside him in the bed.

I didn't disfigure his face, but his chest and midsection looked like a botched spaghetti dinner from Olive Garden. I just laid there and finally fell asleep. It was the best sleep I had had in years. I got up and made something to eat. Then I watched some TV and went back to sleep. This went on for a few days, and Kevin stayed right there. It was the first time in years that my husband had been home for more than twenty-four hours. Kevin started smelling bad at that point, but I couldn't smell anything but peace and satisfaction.

Every time Baby Sis would call, I would tell her that this was just not a good time to come because Kevin was home and we couldn't talk the way would like to. Thank God Baby Sis would call before she'd come. I wouldn't want her to come over and see the mess I'd made.

CHAPTER 11

THE ARREST

I had not showered since that night, and a few days passed before I called the police. After I made the call, I just sat in the kitchen and zoned out. There were lights, screaming, and the officers trying to control the noisy neighbors. That was all I remembered. The police came in. I left the door unlocked. After all, I was the one who had called them. I was at peace. I felt collected and calm as I sat in my kitchen with the same clothes I had worn from that fateful night.

"Ma'am! Ma'am! Are you okay?" the officer said.

She waved two fingers across my eyes to see if I was coherent, but I didn't say anything. "Ma'am, my name is Officer Sanchez. I need to ask you a few questions." I still could not answer. I just sat there and stared into space. I heard everything that was going on. I just couldn't say anything. I could hear Officer Sanchez walking in our room and then running out of the house to vomit. I could see the nosey neighbor peeking in the doorway, trying to figure out what had happened.

There were detectives, police officers, and forensic scientists all around me. I heard one of the officers tell the paramedics that they wouldn't need their services. In my head I chuckled. I felt free even as darkness swept over me. I sat with the stench of a three-day-old murder on me.

Several law enforcement officers asked me questions, but I could not answer. Still, I felt safe. My tongue was nailed to the roof of my mouth. The very next thing I heard was, "Ma'am, you have the right to remain silent." I obeyed every command I was given as I was escorted out of my house. From the corner of my eye, I saw the bloody body bag with my husband's remains and my gift being carried out. I could see my gift through the plastic ziplock bag labeled "Exhibit A."

I was taken to the city jail for questioning, because I wasn't quite a suspect yet. The authorities thought I might be in shock because I wasn't speaking. I was fingerprinted too. Of course, my prints were all over the gift, and I knew that I was going to jail. I really didn't care if I was sentenced to death. I was relieved and free. I was examined by a medical expert and cleaned up. They washed my hair and brushed it. My world seemed different but better. Of course, all the evidence pointed to me, but I still couldn't speak. They all concluded that I was catatonic and in a state of shock.

I felt all the necessary emotions, but the exit point was blocked, so I appeared unremorseful. I had been a regular housewife, but now I had become famous overnight. I was on every local news channel. Everyone wanted to know why this young wife killed her husband and why she wasn't saying a word to defend herself. I wanted deeply to say something, but I just couldn't. I never wanted to be famous. Now I was the hottest thing on the network.

Sadly, Momma and Baby Sis had to hear about me on the news. Since Momma may not remember I was her daughter, I thought she'd be okay. I was sure one person was not going to let this one go easy, and that was Baby Sis. She was going to get to the bottom to this even if it cost her everything.

After being in prison for a month, Baby Sis came to visit me with tears in her eyes. All I did was sit and stare into the air, but she so eagerly wanted to know what happened. She would beg me to answer. I just stared. I would burst into tears because in my heart I wanted to tell her how much I loved her and Momma. I wanted to say that I was really okay because I wasn't getting beaten day in and day out. Baby Sis would then leave in a hurry, and I could hear her crying as she ran down the hallway.

Now that I was the prime suspect, I was moved to maximum security because of the nature of the crime. I was considered crazy, so I was placed in a hospital type jail. Unsure about where I was, all I cared about was the feeling of safety. Baby Sis wrote often, but of course, I couldn't write back. I still couldn't write or speak. Several psychologists would come to question me, but to no avail.

I just could not speak. It was like I was paralyzed and undergoing surgery. I could feel everything but couldn't move or open my mouth to tell the doctor to stop.

But if anyone in this world was going to stay with me through thick and thin, it would be my baby sister. She never gave up on me. Her husband didn't believe her when she tried to tell him that something had driven me to kill my husband. After all, he had never really gotten to know me since Kevin had kept me so isolated from my family. David was a little different from Kevin. He was exactly who he appeared to be. He meant what he said. If he said he was going to do something, he did it, and if he couldn't do it, he would let you know. I only knew David through Baby Sis, but if he was anything different, I would have known. She came to see me one day, and she was uptight because she and David had had a quarrel about me. David just couldn't understand why she insisted that there was more to the story. David felt that I should be left in jail. I had done the crime, and now I had to do my time. He thought Baby Sis should just let it be. She said David thought I'd lost it, and he didn't want her to catch any of my insanity. He was frustrated. He couldn't understand why she kept coming to see me and trying to make sure that I got my untold story out.

But David was sweet. Oh, how he loved Baby Sis. Chelsea is her name. She was a looker too. She and Momma looked like twins. I wasn't the prettiest, but I could make myself up if I worked at it. Everything about Chelsea was pretty. She had thick black hair and perfect skin. When she was little, everyone wanted to take pictures of her because she looked like a doll. Momma would not let everyone take her photo though. Only people she trusted could.

Momma treated us both like we were the most beautiful girls in the world, although we knew who the prettiest was just by the way the world reacted to us in public. One time when we were in high school, Baby Sis and I were walking home. All the boys were looking at her like she was Miss America, and when I said, "Y'all had better stop looking at my baby sister like that," everyone's mouth dropped as if to say, "How are those two related?" At that point, I knew that Momma was just being a good mother and that there was a drastic difference between the way Chelsea and me looked.

I often wondered if Kevin would have beaten and treated Baby Sis like he did me if they had gotten married. Would she have even dated a man like him? Kevin was handsome, but he just didn't have his stuff together. I was just so happy that someone was interested in me. Knowing Baby Sis, she probably would have seen right through his lies and left him alone. Even though I didn't speak, my heart leaped when Baby Sis would come to see me. On this particular day when Baby Sis came to visit me, she began to tell me how she knew something was wrong but just couldn't put her finger on it. She would say, "One day it will all come out." I just looked at her and cried on the inside, saying within myself, "Baby girl, if you only knew." Baby Sis and David always seemed to get along. Even when they would quarrel over me, they would never stay mad forever. I would just listen to Baby Sis because she had to do all the talking. Normally, it was the other way around. During one visit Baby Sis told me she was pregnant. I was leaping for joy inside, and on the outside tears of joy ran down my face. All I could do was lift my hand to stroke her face. I prayed that she could somehow feel how much I loved her.

Before she left, she always said, "One day, sissy, its going to all come out. And when it does, these walls are gonna have to give you up." I thought to myself, *Only God knows*. I had deliberately murdered my husband,

and I did not have any remorse. I belonged where I was. My sleep was good, and my spirits we really high. At least they were high to me. I was never asked to attend my late husband's funeral. People must have figured that wouldn't have been a good idea. I sure would have loved to see him lying there, unable to hurt me or anyone else anymore. That would have been a sight to see.

Maybe it was for the best. After all, he had family who might not have seen things the way I saw them. Actually, I never knew any of his family—not his mother, sister, brother, or father. That should have been another red flag. If only I had known when I had taken him home from the church parking lot.

CHAPTER 12

THE VOICE

Years seemed like days. I felt a peace in my soul. I would speak to God in my heart and tell him that I loved him and confess that I'd done a horrible thing, but then I'd tell him that I still wanted to go to heaven if he would allow me in. Baby Sis gave me a Bible, and I begin to read it from the beginning. I didn't like to leave my room. I enjoyed staying in my room and looking into space. Because of the nature of my crime and my mental state, the staff just let me be. If I didn't want recreation, they wouldn't force me to have recreation.

My meals were sent to my cell. I didn't have a roommate, so I was left alone 90 percent of the day. My meds were given to me in a cup. I flushed those down the toilet on a regular basis. I knew what I was doing, and I knew I wasn't crazy. As I was lying in my room and just staring out of my window, I heard a voice. I sat up, and my heart started beating so fast that I thought I was having a heart attack. The voice knew my name too. "Sonya Watkins, I'm gonna get you outta here!" I looked under my bed and peeped though the hole in my door, but I didn't see anyone. I was so scared that I couldn't sleep now. I really needed those pills that I kept flushing down the toilet. I just sat there waiting for the voice again, but I never heard it again. "Who was that?" I whispered. I didn't think anyone heard me, but someone did. *What did I say that for?* I asked myself.

I could hear the screaming from the cell. "Sophia's home now! She can talk! The dead has arisen!" They had left me alone because I had never talked before, but now everyone wanted to know what had happened. The guards came running down the hall because of the ruckus.

I became famous all over again. This time I was jailhouse famous. The shrinks and doctors were like the paparazzi. Once they knew that I could talk, I had five hundred mics in my face every day. They would ask me a thousand questions, trying to figure out why I had committed murder. I just clammed up again. It was too much drama. Day in and day out, they kept asking those questions. They even gave me a truth serum. That was it for me, so I tapped out. There was this one sassy sistah, that would come to visit me, Dr. Jones. She was sharp, and she didn't talk much. She would just stare at me for a few moments. When she walked, her footsteps echoed with power. I knew it was her when she would walk down the hall. Her head would rock a little and tilt when she had something to say. She'd crack a smile and make a declaration, and that would be it for a while. I'm not sure where she came from, but she had some type of pull. I didn't know if she was an attorney, or counselor. Whatever she was, she was clearly sharp.

Her visits were more on the observant side than anything. Unlike the others, she wouldn't ask me a lot of questions. She would observe and ask maybe one or two questions. During many of the visits, she said nothing to me at all. On many occasions she would check my room for dust and look at my bedsheets. She knew exactly how I made my bed and how I laid my items out. Without any words, she would hold my hands and look me in my eyes. We would stand there in silence, and I just stared right back at her.

One time Dr. Jones aka Mrs. Sassy came, and she wouldn't sit down. She just slowly paced around the room, not looking at me at all. She stared out the window and made this one declaration that stopped my heart. "Sonya Watkins, I'm gonna get you outta here!" I almost fell out of my chair. I burst into tears. That's the voice! Well, it wasn't the voice, but those were the words that I heard. Oh, my God! The voice had said the very same thing. I just wanted to run, but I couldn't move. I couldn't talk either. It was like I had a ton of bricks on my lips.

My heart was beating so fast. Even the guards knew something had happened. My face must have been glowing like Moses's when he came down from the mountaintop. After that visit, I dug out my Bible and reacquainted myself with the Word of God.

It turned out that woman was Dr. Jones. She was a district attorney at one time. She didn't like the way the system worked, so she opened her own law firm. She also went to the church I used to go to, which meant she went to the same church where I had met Kevin. Dr. Jones didn't speak much. She would say what she had to say, and that was that.

I loved it when she visited me, even though I couldn't tell her. Somehow, I figured she knew I really liked her. I felt like I could trust her. If I could talk, I would have told her everything, but I couldn't. Unbeknownst to me at the time, Dr. Jones was researching my case with a fine-tooth comb. She found the doctor that treated me for my so-called car accident and learned that the doctor never believed Kevin's story, but he felt he couldn't step out on a limb as a young doctor just getting his feet wet. If he had been wrong, it could have damaged his career. I felt he knew something wasn't right by the way he kept looking at me back then. He knew the damage to my uterus did not coincide with the story. My hips, legs and pelvis would have been crushed in the accident too. We were both too scared of the outcome to take such a challenge, and I wasn't going to say anything contrary to Kevin's story.

We had a deep soul connection, but we both couldn't speak what was in our hearts. Dr. Jones collaborated with some lawyers to fight for justice. These six law geeks started going through my medical records and spoke to neighborhood residents and some of Kevin's old lovers. They worked Monday through Sunday on my case. My life filled their lives. So many years had passed, and the truth was coming to the light even though I wasn't talking.

The young doctor had finally gotten comfortable with his medicinal practice, so he released my medical records from every visit. He went as far as getting second and third opinions with other doctors. Eventually, they ordered a full-body CAT scan for me. I finally got to leave the confines of the maximum-security facility where I had spent so many years. When I arrived at the hospital, I saw the doctor, but he wasn't so young anymore. However, he was handsome. There I went, lusting again, I thought to myself, *I haven't had this feeling in a long time. Okay, Sonya, put the brakes on. Remember where lusting got you the last time?* Once we completed the tests, the results were staggering. The doctors saw countless broken bones that had healed on their own without medical treatment. They also realized that parts of my liver had been lacerated and my lower ribs were broken and left to heal without medical intervention.

The scan also showed pieces of bone in my gums where he had punched my teeth out. The lawyers soon discovered that an accident report had never been filed at the police station for my initial hospitalization and that there was no evidence of a damaged vehicle. They knew that with the bruises that I had sustained in the so-called accident, there should have been a totaled vehicle. God was really speaking on my behalf.

Every now and then, Dr. Jones would come by and say, "Sonya, you have got to work with me. Open your mouth!" She'd wait for a few minutes, but she never gave me a lot of time to answer. This went on for weeks. At times she wanted to choke me, but what good would that have done? I was already silent.

In my mind, I was dying to tell her that I had been abused every day, but I just couldn't bring myself say anything to help myself. It was almost like I wanted to be there. I knew what I had done, but on the other hand, I felt like I had been dealt a bad hand and that I deserved compensation. During Dr. Jones's visits, she would never disclose her finding. She would just tell me that I had to talk. Something deep down inside of Dr. Jones told her that something was not right. She really was the Christian I should have been. After all, we had attended the same church.

I would pray and ask God to help me and to give me the ability to speak again. There was so much evidence that I was being abused. How could nobody have known? It turned out that Kevin had a record of domestic violence in another state. His first wife was lucky that she had reported him. He had beaten her so bad that he was incarcerated and she was granted a divorce. He had an order of protection against him, so he left the state. He would stalk and harass her. Thankfully, all of this was documented. Praise God! I didn't feel like a hopeless case anymore. I began to believe that God was with me now and that all things were going to work for my good.

The investigation took a while, but Dr. Jones pulled every string she could to build a defense case for me. She even went to God about me. She asked him to give her guidance and to send her people who would provide concrete evidence. For once in my adult life, I began to believe in the God that I wanted to serve. I felt so small because I was not true to God, but he was so faithful and true to me. I knew the truth. God never changed. He was always awesome whether we chose to see it or not. I began to reflect on the days that Kevin would beat and verbally abuse me. I was still alive, and now I had hope. What a wonderful God.

Although Kevin's mom had to bury him, I still felt that I was going to be okay. Then there was a break in the case. One of Kevin's former lovers told a member of Dr. Jones's squad that he had a bad temper and would often tell her that if he came home and she didn't have dinner ready, he would stomp the shit out of her. He even told her how he had felt so bad for beating me to a pulp one day and hoped I didn't have to go to the hospital again. She also noted that he had told her all of this when he was drunk. She put a special emphasis on how he would tell her these things so that she would know that he loved her and not me.

Momma used to say, "If he beats her, what makes you think he won't beat you?" People might think this former lover was dumb, but then they'd have to put me in the same category. But these people loved Kevin just like I loved him. No matter what he did, said, or didn't have, I loved him. He was handsome and charming—at least at first.

Of course, Dr. Jones could have turned the tables and made that woman an accomplice, but the godly part in that woman wouldn't allow her to do that. It didn't make sense for both of us to be tormented because of Kevin. So many accounts about Kevin losing his temper with the many women he was sleeping with surfaced. I often wondered why their stories were getting out and mine was stuck in my throat.

The more I prayed, the more I began to mumble and pray in a very low voice. I began speaking in my heavenly language. We were taught how to speak in tongues at an early age. Baby Sis and I loved to try to beat each other when it came to speaking in tongues just to see whose speech sounded more like a foreign language.

CHAPTER 13

THE TRIAL

The day finally arrived, and I prayed to God that I would be able open my mouth to speak. I knew I had the ability to talk, but I wasn't sure if I was going to able to speak about Kevin. I walked into the courtroom, and I expected to see angry faces; however, I didn't see that at all. Their faces were pleasant. They just stared at me, and I could hear their whispers as they looked me up and down. I couldn't quite imagine what they were looking at. Dr. Jones had met with Baby Sis to get some photos of me before I had met Kevin, and she also retrieved pictures of me after the so-called car accident.

My God, when they showed the pictures of me on the big screen, all I could do was cry. He had beaten me so bad that the pictures looked like they were of two different women from two different eras. I looked out into courtroom, and I saw Momma. She didn't know who was on trial. I saw Baby Sis and David too. Even he looked like he had hope for me.

There were others I knew and some I didn't know, but I felt something down in my spirit. That voice had really been the voice of God, and He had my back. Although Momma didn't remember a lot, she knew the Lord, and He never let her prayers fall to the ground. We all knew that only a prayer from Momma could get her baby out of this mess. It turned out that Baby Sis and Dr. Jones had discovered some evidence that was pivotal to my case. They had spoken with some nosey neighbors.

They knew when he beat me, when he brought women home, and when he slept around the neighborhood. Heck, they even remembered when I first brought him home after a few months. My neighbors could tell you when I went to church and when I stopped going to church because I had fallen into sin. Thank God for nosey neighbors. One older lady took the stand and said, "I never could understand what a pretty girl like that was doing with such a sleaze bucket." I looked around the courtroom before realizing that she was calling me pretty. Surely, she must have been talking about the other women he had brought home when I was working. Maybe she had gotten me confused with one of his many women. No, she was talking about me. I just couldn't see it then, and as sure as the day was long, I couldn't see it now.

It was a long trial. I was tired, and the jurors were tired too. When it was time for me to take the stand, I heard someone whisper, "Did you see her leg? It drags. She has been through so much!"

"That poor baby!" someone said. I could hear sighs of sympathy and compassion, which was not what I had expected.

When I began to speak, everything came out. When the wells finally dried up, the judge said, "Thank you, Mrs. Watkins. You may take your seat."

"Your Honor!" the prosecuting attorney said. "I have just one question for the defendant if I may."

I paused and breathed heavy and said, "All right!"

"Mrs. Watkins, please take the stand again." the judge said.

I went back and sat down, and then I heard the question that rang in everyone's heart. "Mrs. Watkins, why didn't you say anything earlier? Why are you a singing bird now?" As the prosecuting attorney, he was trying to be shrewd, lawless, and heartless.

Tears rolled down my eyes, and I just looked at him and said, "I didn't think anyone would believe me." And I hung my head back down.

The prosecuting attorney looked at me as if he made

the most horrific mistake of his career and just looked at me and said, "That's all, Mrs. Watkins. Thank you."

As I went to my seat, the air felt thick. It was so still in the room you could hear stomachs growling. None of us had eaten in hours. The judge finally said, "Court's adjourned. We'll meet back here tomorrow at nine o'clock tomorrow morning."

I couldn't sleep that night. I thought about getting released, but I also felt mixed emotions. What if I was found guilty? I couldn't eat. Morning finally came, and I then walked in the courtroom. Immediately, I saw my sister, my mom, and different lady.

I took my seat, and they began to murmur. I couldn't tell what they were saying, but I knew they were talking about me. The gavel came down, and the judge said, "Order in the court!" The whole place got silent. When all the jurors came in and sat down, the judge said, "We will now read the verdict."

One of the jurors stood up and said, "Your honor, in the case of *Watkins v. the State of Georgia* in the account of the murder of Mr. Kevin Watkins, the court finds Mrs. Sonya Watkins ..." It was like the world stopped for a day. I got so dizzy I could hardly keep my composure. I didn't think my heart could take much more. The juror continued, "Not guilty of first-degree murder!" My heart stopped for a moment. The whole court sighed with relief. Was I a free woman? Was this a dream?

I was surrounded by so many people who were on my side, and my baby sister then said, "I told you that one day it would all come out in the wash!" She shook her head, tears of joy running down her cheeks.

Then that strange lady who knew me—even though I didn't recognize her—came over to me, grabbed me and said, "Baby, I'm so, so sorry."

I just looked at her strangely and asked her, "Ma'am, you have nothing to be sorry for. I really don't know who you are."

"No, baby, but I know who you are. I'm Mrs. Betty Watkins, Kevin's mother." I wanted to die all over again. I was hugging the woman whose son I had murdered.

"Ma'am, I am sorry. Will you please forgive me?" I said.

"You don't have to apologize for anything, honey. My son abused every woman he had. I looked at you on that stand, and I knew that if you had not done something, he would have killed you." We hugged until we felt a release.

The day came, and the time was nigh for me to leave the place that I would have called home for the rest of my life. As I was being processed, I retrieved all my items and found Dr. Jones and her team. I was so overwhelmed that these young lawyers in town had worked so diligently to present my case. We greeted one another, and when I got to Dr. Jones, she held me in her arms and said, "Sonya Watkins, I told you I was gonna get you out!"

I knew that God would use people to carry out his wishes. I just grinned and said, "Won't he do it?"

We all walked out of the building with the guards, and that's when I saw Baby Sis and David waiting for me to come outside. Surprisingly, David hugged me and said, "I'm glad the truth came out."

I thought to myself, *You thought I deserved to be in jail, but now that the truth came out, you're all in my face. Naw, I know everyone had every right to feel the way they did about me, good or bad.*

The only sad part about my reunion was the fact that Momma wasn't there, but Mrs. Betty was. She made her way to me, and then she began to take my things out of my hand. She said, "Baby, please come stay with me. I know you have family, but I would love for you to come stay with me. Let me make amends for all the things my son has done to you." I looked at my sister, and she gave me that "It's okay" nod.

Then I said, "Yes, ma'am, but first, I have to go see my mama."

"Why, of course, baby girl. You can see your mother anytime. I'm not stealing you. I just want you to live with me until you get back on your feet."

I went home with Baby Sis and David so that I could see Momma. When I walked in, she knew who

I was and called me by my name—Sonya. I kneeled down by her side and just allowed her to hold my face in her hands as we both cried. "Sunny, my little Sunny, I knew you were coming back. I knew because God told me He was going to bring my baby home." I looked at Baby Sis, and she just shrugged her shoulders. Neither of us had any idea that Momma knew anything about my tragic marriage.

As confused as I was, I asked Momma, "You knew?"

She just held my face as said, "Baby, God knew."

Perplexed and angry, I got up from beside her and pulled Baby Sis into the other room. "Are you crazy? How … how could you be so careless?"

Baby Sis was just as confused as I was. "Sunny, I didn't. I promise I didn't say anything to Momma. Sunny, I promise!"

"Are you sure? Not even talking around Momma?"

Baby sis pleaded with me. She said she had never spoken a word to or around her about my situation. I knew my sister wasn't a liar, and she was never negligent either.

The longer I stayed, the more Momma's mental state regressed back into dementia. It was as if she came back just for a little while for me. *Thank you, Jesus*, I thought. I talked with Baby Sis and told her all the things that I wanted to do, including going to church, going shopping, and eat at all the restaurants on the row. We laughed and cried. David allowed us to have our time together. He would stroll by and peek in the room, and I could see him flash a knowing smile because his baby was so happy to be with her big sister.

"Hey, Dave!" I said and beckoned him to come to the room. "Sit down." I tapped the bed so that he could sit with us. "Dave, I want you to know something. If you don't already know, Baby Sis knew that something was wrong the whole time. But I didn't know how dangerous Kevin was, and I didn't want you or Baby Sis to get involved with him or his demonic antics."

David began to weep. He didn't know what to believe, and I truly understand just like the Bible says in the book of Matthew 13:24 when Jesus talks about the wheat and the tares. Jesus said you have to let them grow together until it matures then only will you be able to tell the wheat from the tare. Sometimes in life situations may look like one thing; but when in time if you wait the truth will come out. "Dave, you don't have to be ashamed. I did kill my husband. Yes, I knew what I was doing when I planned it. What everyone didn't know, what I couldn't explain was that he beat me beyond what the trial could reveal. David …" I began to choke up, but I continued, "I thought that I had no other recourse but to take his life. If he would have beaten me one more time, I would have died. You know the story now David." I grabbed his hand and said, "Now Dave, if you even remotely try that with my sister, I'll gladly go back to prison."

The air was dry, and his and Baby Sis's eyes were as big as plates. Then I busted out laughing, and David and Baby Sis took a much-needed exhale. We all just laughed and chatted until the wee hours of the morning.

I gave Mrs. Betty a call the next day to set up a time for her to pick me up and start our new journey. When she picked me up from Baby Sis's house, she came in a very nice car. I was reluctant to get in the car with her, but I did.

"Mrs. Watkins, thanks so much."

"No, baby, thank you for allowing me to serve you."

"I'm not sure what you mean, ma'am."

"Baby, you just don't know how I prayed for you."

"For me?" I replied, confused. "How did you know about me?"

"Well, baby, Kevin told me he had gotten married. We never talked much because he thought I was always against him, but the truth was that I didn't approve of his abusive behavior." I just sat silently and listened as we drove an hour and a half to the countryside. "Kevin's father was abusive to me and Kevin. He'd beat Kevin so bad that I knew I had to get my child out of that house quick, but I was too late. Kevin got his dad's gun and shot his father in the chest." I was shocked as I listened to the horrific story of Kevin's upbringing.

I cried on the inside because that explained his behavior. "How old was Kevin when he killed his dad?"

"Oh, he was around ten or eleven. We had so many cases of abuse reported from the school. Those reported cases kept Kevin out of juvenile detention but not out of therapy. After that ordeal, Kevin became very introverted. Since Kevin's father had a very good insurance policy and since he was murdered, they had no problem paying us the full 1.5 million dollars." My eyes were wide, but I continued to listen. "So I took the money and all our savings and moved out to the country where Kevin could get some peace of mind.

"Unfortunately, that didn't help. Kevin was the only child, and living so far away from the city with his mother alone may not have been the best way to nurture a son who killed his father. I noticed as he became older, he lacked social skills. It was difficult for him to make and keep friends, especially girls. He would beat them up because they wouldn't like him, and he'd do the cruelest things to them just because they didn't want to date him." We continued to drive. The scenery was simple and beautiful, but the story was making me nauseous.

I was not beaten because I was ugly or God didn't care about me anymore. I was beaten because Kevin had issues and because I loved him more than I loved myself. "Mrs. Watkins, I'm sorry to interrupt."

"No, no, you're fine."

"I noticed you said it was only you and Kevin. You didn't have any other children?"

"I was pregnant several times twice prior to Kevin and once after Kevin was born; but ..." I saw a flood beginning in her eyes. "Kevin's father and I would fight so much I'd miscarry. So when Kevin was born and I lost another baby, I couldn't allow this tyrant to take the only thing that had survived."

There I was sitting in the passenger seat with the mother of the man I had killed, and she wanted to take care of me. Or did she have some ulterior motive? *Sunny, stop!* I thought to myself. *This is not karma coming for me.*

"So Mrs. Betty, what happened to the women when he finally was able to date?"

"Well, none of them went well. They were all beaten by Kevin, but they all left him. The one who was at your trial actually pressed charges and had an order of protection filed against him.

"He would only tell me he was in a relationship. He'd never tell me when it started or when it ended. Our relationship went sour when he beat his very first wife. Her mother just happened to be a good friend of mine. In his mind, I was more interested in not losing a friend than taking his side. That was so far from the truth. I came to find out that Kevin would tell them how he would kill them and get away with it like he had done before.

"His case was sealed, but of course, he made the news because he was the young boy who had killed his father. Plus his father was a … police officer." Mrs. Betty hung her head slightly down. She was driving, but she was also ashamed. She had the law in her bed, beating her and her kid, and her child was a bragging murderer too. That was what Momma had now—a daughter who was a murderer. "I'm so sorry, Sonya. Would you like to stop at the store and get some personal items?"

"Yes, ma'am; but I—"

"I know you don't have any money, honey. You just got out of jail."

"Yes, ma'am," I answered, with my head down.

We stopped at Walmart, and we both realized we still had a ways to go before we made it home. I grabbed some personal items and a few outfits, and then we were back in the car. "Are you hungry, Sonya?"

"Yes, ma'am!"

"Well, what would you like to eat?"

"Not sure. Anything would do."

"Well, I know this nice little spot I can take you to. We can call in an order and bring it home and eat."

"Sounds good to me," I said, feeling a tad bit of

freedom. Sometimes you can better understand the fruit if you know the root. Just listening to Mrs. Betty helped me to understand why all this had transpired.

We arrived at the cottage in the countryside. The woods were so serene. We drove up to this beautiful house and pulled up in front of the door. I gasped and said, "You live here by yourself?"

"Yes, ever since Kevin left, I just stay here all by my lonesome. He would stay with me in between women, but I haven't seen him since he married you."

I was baffled again because I remembered taking Kevin to his own apartment. "So you didn't know he had his own apartment?"

"Yes, I always helped him get back on his feet whenever he'd come back home, but after he met you and got married, I barely heard from Kevin."

We unpacked my things, and I got settled in. Then I took a tour of this luxurious home. I had never known a black family with a pool. They weren't poor, but a pool? "Sonya! Sonya!" Mrs. Betty called.

"Ma'am!"

"Come in here and sit with me for a while."

"Yes, ma'am, I'm coming."

It was clear she hadn't had a visitor in years. I was the only joy she'd had in a long time. I figured I could accommodate. "Have a seat. I want to go over some stuff with you." Nervously, I sat across from her at her dinette table in the kitchen. "I told you I was praying for you as soon as Kevin told me he'd gotten married. I knew you were in trouble because I knew my son and his history with women.

"Tomorrow first thing in the morning, I need you to come with me. I need to make some things right."

"Ma'am …"

"No, I insist."

"Yes, ma'am." I agreed reluctantly, not really knowing what she was going to do tomorrow. Only God knew.

The morning came, and I woke up refreshed. I had not slept so much since the day before I saw Kevin in church. This sleep was better than any of my other peaceful sleeps in my life. I really wasn't sure what the day was going to bring, but I was ready to face it. I came into the kitchen, and Mrs. Watkins looked like a rich white woman. She had so many diamonds. We hopped in the car without eating, but we stopped at a local diner. After we ate, we went to the bank. I wasn't sure what to expect, but I came in anyway. The manager was waiting for us, and I felt famous again. The bank staff smiled and greeted us. I really didn't know what to make of all the hype. "Mrs. Watkins, Mrs. Watkins, this way." The manager extended his hand for us to enter into his chic office. I sat down and stared at all the rich decor around me as he laid all these papers in front of me. I glanced over them, and my jaw dropped. I started crying almost immediately. "Is there a problem?" the manager asked, but he knew exactly what I was feeling. I could tell from the knowing smirk on his face.

Mrs. Betty just sat there as if she had nothing to do with what was about to happen. I finally got myself together enough to find the amount of money that was being signed over to me from Kevin's policy. Mrs. Betty had made me the beneficiary of her estate. I had gone from rags to riches in matter of forty-two hours. I was speechless and had no idea how to swallow this pill. When God said in the Holy Bible that he will pour you out a blessing you won't be able to receive, I know what that means now. I could not wrap my mind around this. I had walked in penniless, and I left the bank as a woman who would never have to work another day in her life.

CHAPTER 14

NEW BEGINNINGS

I had to write my life story as an advocate for domestic violence and a brand-new woman. Unfortunately, Mrs. Betty had stage-four cancer, and months after I moved in with her, she passed away. I kept the property and renovated the house to help battered women and their children recover. I really didn't have time to get myself together before I was back at the bank and signing more paperwork. I gave Mrs. Betty the best funeral service that anyone in that community had ever had. She was well loved, and she knew Jesus. The church was packed. Momma, Baby Sis, and David came to pay their respects. God has perfect timing. He knows exactly what He's doing, and no matter how we think we may have missed the mark, God always shows us that He knows best.

Momma was still slipping in and out of reality, but she managed to come in just enough to give me a word from God. I purchased a home for Baby Sis and

Dave, and I opened up a legal fund with Dr. Jones for individuals who needed lawyers but could not afford to retain one. Of course, I took care of my church, and I also took care of Sunny. I bought a new set of teeth— implants to be exact. I had a few surgeries to correct my broken nose and realign my jaw. I even bought myself some boobs. I couldn't help but laugh afterward. I'd always wanted full boobs. I didn't go too big, just a little bigger and firmer. I looked in the mirror, and all I could do was thank the Lord that I didn't look like what I had been through.

Today I can honestly say that I am a faithful member of the best church in the world. Yes, I attend every service that we have. On one Sunday in particular, I was walking to my car, just happy to be in God's army, and I heard this man's voice. He said, "Ma'am, can I walk you to your car?"

I started to turn around, and I wanted to say, "Do you know what happened to the last guy I met in the parking lot?" But instead I just politely said, "No, sir, I'm good. You have a blessed day." And I kept moving. I am not desperate or needy. My time with God is more than life, and I am reaching the world with the gospel of Jesus and breaking the chains of violence and abusive relationships.

I'm not saying I don't ever want to get remarried; however, right now I'm on a mission for God, and

I'm not getting sidetracked for anyone. I'm going all the way with God. Falling into sin almost cost me my life, but God gave me a second chance. I thank God for sparing my life. He gave me a better life, a more abundant life. For that I will be forever grateful. I pray for everyone that is in an abusive relationship, whether a man or woman. I pray that God will give you the courage and resources to get out. When you come out, my prayer is that you will never return and will always give God all the glory. In Jesus's name, amen.

Now that's a testimony!